I0618385

THE SCIENTISTS REVOLT

THE SCIENTISTS REVOLT

EDGAR RICE BURROUGHS

AND RAY PALMER

WILDSIDE PRESS

Originally published in July, 1939 in
Fantastic Adventures magazine.
No record of copyright renewal found.

Published by Wildside Press, LLC
www.wildsidebooks.com

PROLOGUE

2190 A.D.

A small pane in the leaded glass of the Pent House Palace atop the tallest building in Assuria tinkled to the study floor as the bullet embedded itself in the ebony paneling behind the Science Ruler.

"Guns!" he exclaimed. "They must have raided the museums. Even with ancient guns, they attack the Science Palace. How their hate has misled them!" He turned ruefully to survey the panel. "My great grand-sire brought that from ancient Paris, over a hundred years ago, Sanders—'so fleet the works of man, back to their earth again, ancient and holy things fade like a dream'."

As the Science Ruler spoke, his companion crossed the room quickly. "Come, sir!" he cried, "we must leave this apartment. That shot was intended for you."

The Science Ruler shook his head sadly. "But for my wife, I could have wished the fellow had been a better marksman."

"And your son, Alexander," Sanders reminded him.

"It might make it easier for him," replied the Science Ruler. "It is I they hate. My people hate me, Sanders— my people, whom I love and to whom I have tried to be a father. But them I cannot blame. They have been deceived by lies. It is toward those who knew the truth, who lived closest to me, and for whom I did the most that I feel any bitterness. Every day they are deserting me, Sanders—the rats and the sinking ship. I am sure of only a few of you—I could count my friends tonight upon the fingers of one hand."

Michael Sanders, Minister of War, bowed his head, for the Science Ruler had spoken the truth and there was no denial to be made.

It was the first of May preceding that historic second which wiped the science dynasty from the rule of Assuria. For a month the Science family had virtually been prisoners in the summer palace upon the outskirts of the Capitol, but they had been unmolested, and their personal safety had seemed reasonably assured until this morning.

For years the voice of the agitator and the malcontent had been heard with increasing emphasis throughout the length and breadth of the Country. "We are slaves to science" was the text from which they preached. During the early weeks of April, the Capitol had been a hotbed of revolution which had rapidly merged into the chaos of anarchy. The people had grievances, but no leader—they had only agitators, who could arouse, but not control.

And then had come this first of May, when the rabble from the low quarters of the city, drunk with liquor and with blood lust, had derided the weaklings at the head of the revolution, and screaming for blood and loot, had marched upon the Science palace with the avowed intention of assassinating the Science family.

All that day they had howled and hooted about the palace, held in check only by a single military unit which had remained loyal to the Scientists—the Foreign Corps, recruited among foreigners, and with few exceptions, similarly officered.

After a moment's silence, the Science Ruler spoke again.

"What do you suppose started them today?" he asked. "What brought this mob to the palace?"

"They heard last night of the birth of your son," replied Sanders. "They pretend to see in that fact a menace to what they are pleased to call The New Freedom—that is why they are here, sir."

"You think they want the lives of my wife and son, as well as my life?"

Sanders bowed. "I am sure of it, sir."

"That must be prevented at all cost," said the Science Ruler.

"I had thought of removing them from the palace," replied Sanders, "but that would be difficult, even were it possible to move your wife, which the physicians assure me must not be done. But there is just a faint possibility that we may be able to remove the baby boy. I have given the matter a great deal of thought, sir. I have a plan. It entails risk, but on the other hand, to permit the boy to remain in this building another twelve hours would, I am confident, prove fatal."

"Your plan, Sanders, what is it?" demanded the Scientist.

"For the past month the officers of the Foreign Corps have been quartered within the building. Several of them are married men, and their wives are here with them. One of these women, the wife of a Lieut. Donovan, gave birth to a son two days since. She is a strong and healthy young woman and could be moved without materially endangering her health. For all the people know, she may have had twins."

The Science Ruler elevated his brows. "I see," he said, "but how could she pass out with the infants? No one may escape."

"But they do daily, sir," replied Sanders. "The building is filled with traitors. Not a day passes but that several desert to the enemy. We are close pressed. Only a miracle can save the Foreign Corps from absolute extermination. It would not seem strange, then, to the revolutionists, should Lt. Donovan desert to them for the sake of the safety of his wife and children."

For several minutes the Science Ruler stood with bowed head, buried in thought. Then: "Call Danard," he said, "and we will send for this Lt. Donovan."

"Perhaps I had better go myself," said Sanders. "The fewer who know of what we intend, the safer will be the secret."

"I have implicit confidence in Danard," replied the Science Chief. "He has served me faithfully for many years."

"Pardon, sir," said Sanders, "but the occasion is one of such tremendous moment that I would be untrue to the trust you repose in me were I to remain silent—sir,

I fear Danard, I mistrust him, I have no confidence in him."

"Why?"

"I could substantiate no charge against him," replied Sanders, "or I should have preferred charges long ago, yet..."

"Poof!" exclaimed the Science Ruler. "Danard would die for me. Bring him, please."

Sanders moved toward the radio call, but with his hand upon the switch he turned again.

"I beg of you, sir, to let me go instead."

The elder man replied with an imperious gesture toward the radio call, and Sanders gave the signal.

A few moments later, Paul Danard, the Science Ruler's valet, entered the chamber. He was a slender, dark man, apparently in his early thirties. His eyes were large and dreamy and set rather too far apart, while, in marked contrast to them, were his thin, aquiline nose and his straight and bloodness lips. He awaited in silence the will of his master, who stood scrutinizing him closely, as though for the first time he had seen the face of the man before him. Presently, however, the Science Ruler spoke.

"Danard," he said, "you've served me faithfully for many years. I have implicit confidence in your loyalty, and because of that I am going to place within your hands tonight the future of Assuria and the safety of my son."

The man bowed low. "My life is yours to command," he replied.

"Good. The mob seeks my life and that of my wife, and of Alexander. Even if I could leave the palace, I would not. My wife, on account of her condition, cannot, but Michael believes that we can smuggle the boy away, where he may remain in safety and seclusion until the deluded people have recovered from the madness which grips them now."

Michael Sanders, watching intently the face of the valet, saw reflected there no emotion which might arouse the slightest suspicion, as the Science Ruler outlined the plan which might cheat the revolutionists of the fruit of their endeavor.

Twenty minutes later Danard returned with Lt. Terrance Donovan, a young Irish soldier of fortune who had been a Lieutenant in the Foreign Corps for better than a year.

Michael explained the plan to the officer.

"The most difficult part," he concluded, "will be in obtaining safe escort for your wife and the two infants through the revolutionists who surround the building, but that is a chance we must take, for in their present mood they will spare no one once they gain access to the building, which now can be but a matter of hours.

"Once you have gained the city, remain in hiding until your wife's strength is equal to travel, then leave the country. Go to America, where funds will be sent you periodically for the care and education of the boy. From time to time you will receive instructions from us, but you will make no reports unless requested, nor attempt in any way to communicate with us, for only by maintaining the utmost secrecy may we hope to preserve the boy from the vengeance of the revolutionists. To prevent suspicion from attaching to you in any way upon the other side, you must pursue some calling that may at least partially account for your income.

"His father, his mother, Danard, your wife, yourself, and I are the only people who will know the identity of your second twin. No other must ever know until you receive authoritative word from Assuria that the time is ripe for his return to his people. Not even the boy himself must know that he is other than your son. Do you understand fully, and do you accept the commission?"

Donovan inclined his head in assent.

"We are placing in your hands the fate of Assuria," said the Science Ruler; "God grant that you may be true to the trust imposed upon you."

"I shall not fail you, sir," replied the Irishman.

Twenty-four hours later, the rabble overcame the remaining guards and forced its way into the Science building. The fate of the Science Ruler and his wife is not known—their bodies were never found. The rage of the revolutionists when they discovered that the infant son had been spirited away was unbounded. But all this is history. If you are interested in it, I recommend to you *The Last Days of the Scientists*[1], by Michael

1   Late in the twenty-first century, all of Europe became involved in a war from which emerged a scientific power that ruled

Sanders, large 12mo, illus., 529 pgs., G. Strake, Ltd., London.

It was the sixteenth of May, two weeks after the fall of the Science Rule, that a tiny, muffled figure, with a weight at its feet, dropped from the stratosphere liner *Colossic* bound for New York. The Atlantic, below, received it. Watching, with tragic eyes, stood a young Irishman. At his side, sobbing softly, his wife clutched a little baby tightly to her breast.

---

the whole continent with an iron hand. It was not a dictatorial, or an unjust rule, since by scientific means, the lot of the people was materially bettered. Under the Science Rule, the country grew prosperous, and it seemed that happiness should certainly have been the lot of the people. But instead, there was constant murmuring against the rule of man by science, for it was a fact that machines did the real thinking behind the government. Robots took the place of pilots in stratosphere planes, industry became a mass of entangling robot factories, and severe economical upheavals resulted.

However, each time, balance was restored, at least to the financial structure of the nation. But morally, the people became undermined. They had too much leisure time. In short, science had come to a continent whose people were not intellectually ready for it. They seethed beneath its irksome perfection. They yearned for something, but they knew not what. And, finally, came revolt. Machine was turned against machine, and as is the case with machines, when the human nerve center is cut, chaos resulted.

Driven to retreat when power beams failed, the Foreign Corps finally succumbed to such ancient weapons as rifles and flame guns. A few short days of fierce fighting and the Science Rule was at an end, perhaps forever on the European continent.

Once more Europe returned to its ancient ways, but whether they would follow the lead of still American America, the ancient, but still young in spirit, democracy, is for future historians to record. In America, science serves, it does not rule.—Excerpt from "The Last Days of the Scientists."

CHAPTER I

Twenty-Two Years Later

"'Your Ma is a very sick woman, Mackie."

The older man, sitting at his desk, did not raise his eyes to his son as he spoke, and the other knew that it was because he feared to reveal the emotion that lay behind them and thus give the boy greater cause for apprehension.

"I guessed as much when I got your message, Dad." As he spoke, Macklin Donovan, arose. Walking to his father's side he laid his hand affectionately and sympathetically upon the broad shoulder of the strato-police lieutenant. "May I see her?" he asked.

"That is all, Mackie—just see her," replied his father. "She won't know you. The doctor has ordered absolute quiet."

The younger man nodded, and together they tiptoed their way upstairs to a room on the second floor.

When they returned to the den again there was a hint of moisture on the lashes of both men.

"How did you find me?" asked the younger man. "Through the department?"

"Yes. I telephoned Washington. Your chief told me where you were."

"I am still on the Thorn case. It's got us guessing. No one in the department believes Mr. Thorn to be more than a visionary philanthropist with conservative socialistic leanings.

CHAPTER II

Murder in the Dark

It was after one o'clock the following morning before they returned from supper and dancing at one of the city's popular sky gardens. Greeves admitted them. As she passed him, Nariva Saran raised her brows questioningly, and the butler replied with an almost imperceptible inclination of his head. Neither act would have been noticeable to other than specially trained senses— such as Donovan's. It was his business to notice such trivial occurrences, and this one did not escape him. He was puzzled and vexed—vexed with himself that he could still doubt Nariva Saran's connection with the band of conspirators that he felt he was at last closing in upon after weeks of seemingly fruitless effort.

He had always suspected Saran and at first had assumed that the Assurian's daughter was criminally connected with the band of which her father was a part. Reasoning from this premise, it was not strange that he should seek to ingratiate himself with the girl, that through her he might gain the knowledge he sought. To this end, he sought her companionsip. The result had been that not only had he been unable to connect her with any of the activities that he believed chargeable to the band under investigation, but he had fallen hopelessly in love with her.

After a few moments' desultory conversation in which no one seemed interested, Miss Thorn announced her intention of retiring—a suggestion that evidently met with the approval of the others, who, with sleepy "Good nights," ascended the stairway to their several chambers.

Fifteen minutes later, Greeves made the rounds of the lower floor, turning off all the lights with the exception of a small night lamp in the front hallway and a second small lamp in the library, which was the last room to which he gave his attention. Instead of returning to the servants' stairway at the rear of the penthouse, which he should have used in going to his room on the fourth floor, he ascended the main stairway from the library. He left a light on the landing about half way up the stairs, but shut off all those in the hallway on the second floor, which was, however, slightly illuminated by the light from the landing.

These duties attended to, he paused for a moment in the center of the hall, apparently listening. He looked quickly first in one direction and then in the other, after which, seemingly satisfied, he ascended the second flight of steps to the third floor, where were located the apartments of the family. Ordinarily a small passenger elevator was used to reach the upper floors, but this was temporarily out of commission while undergoing its annual summer overhauling during the absence of the family at Three Gables. From the third floor, a single flight of stairs led to the servants' quarters on the floor above.

This stairway was near the rear end of the third floor hallway. Directly opposite it was a small, dark closet wherein were kept a various assortment of brooms, brushes, mops, dusters, vacuum cleaners, and similar paraphernalia.

Greeves turned out all but a single light in the third floor hall, walked to the foot of the stairway, paused, listened, and then, turning quickly, crossed the hall silently, opened the door of the dark closet entered it and closed the door after him.

Macklin Donovan had gone directly to his room, removed his dinner coat, tie, and collar, and sat down to smoke and read at a table near one of the open windows which overlooked the small garden in the rear of the house. Outside this window was a narrow iron balcony identical with those outside every other window on this floor, both front and rear. These balconies did not connect with those adjacent to them, being separated by a space of about three feet. Except for the lights of the vast city far below, and the giant twin tower a mile away, the penthouse might have been on a country estate.

Macklin's back was toward the open window and he was facing in the direction of the door leading into the hallway. He was not particularly interested in the book he was reading—it did not hold his attention. It was better than nothing, however, in assisting him to pass the time until the household slumbered, for he had a suspicion that something might transpire thereafter that would prove of interest to him and to his chief in Washington.

He had been sitting thus for about an hour when his eyes alighted upon a folded paper lying on the threshold partially inside the room. It had not been there a moment before, of that he was positive. There had been no sound—the paper had not been there one minute—the next minute it had. That was all there was to it.

In the instant that he discovered the thing, he leaped quickly toward the door with the intention of throwing it open; but before his hand touched the knob, he thought better of his contemplated act and, instead, stooped and picked up the paper. Whoever put it there did not want to be seen. Perhaps it would be better to humor him, temporarily at least.

Standing near the door, he opened the message and read its contents, after which he was glad that he had not yielded to his first impulse to rush into the hall in an effort to discover the messenger. The note was in a feminine hand and read: "Mackie: Please come to my room at quarter past two. I have something to tell you. Do not come before," and it was signed with the initials "N.S."

Donovan's right palm went to the back of his neck in a characteristic gesture of perplexity. It wasn't like Nariva—she wasn't the sort of girl that would ask a man to her room at that hour of the morning—unless— ah, that was it! She wanted to tell him something that she didn't dare tell him before Saran. It must be that.

It must be something urgent. Whatever it was, it was all right; he could trust her—of that he was quite sure.

He glanced at his watch. It lacked about five minutes to quarter past. He went to his dressing room, buttoned on his collar, adjusted his tie, and slipped into his dinner coat.

Before leaving his room, he turned to his dresser, from which he took a needle pistol.[2] He was on the point of slipping it into a hip pocket when he hesitated, and then, with a shrug, replaced it in the dresser and closed the drawer.

Walking toward the hall door, his glance fell upon the table. He came to an abrupt stop and, wheeling, took a hurried survey of the room, for propped against the reading lamp was a square blue envelope that had not been there when he had quitted the room a few minutes before. Snatching it up, he saw his own initials crudely printed upon its face. The flap, which was but freshly sealed, he tore open, revealing an ordinary square correspondence card, upon which was printed in the same rude hand a single word: BEWARE!

A frown creased Donovan's brow. His hall door was locked. He glanced toward the open window and then quickly at his watch. It was exactly quarter past two. Slipping the blue envelope and the card into his pocket, he crossed the room to the hall door. As he laid his hand upon the knob, the faint report of a needle pistol came to his ears, followed almost immediately by the

---

2   A needle pistol is a small, compact weapon, like an ancient automatic. It fires a tiny, needle-shaped pellet, using compressed air as its propelling force.

sound of a body falling, and the piercing shriek of a woman.

Throwing the door open, Donovan stepped out into the hall and ran quickly toward the front of the house— the direction from which the sounds had come. At the head of the stairs leading to the library, he stumbled over a huddled heap covered by a dressing gown. A few feet farther along the hall was Nariva Saran's room on one side and, across from it, that occupied by the fastidious Mrs. Glassock and her daughter.

From the position of the body, Donovan's police instinct sensed almost intuitively the fact that the needle could have been fired from inside Nariva's room, but not from the Glassock room. Too, it might also have been fired from the doorway of the room occupied by John Saran. But from the direction that the doors of the various rooms opened, it could most easily have been fired from Nariva's, had the door been opened not more than an inch, by one standing concealed within.

Some of these things came to him as suspicions at the moment, to be verified by investigation later. But above all else there loomed above him like a hideous specter the appalling fact that the needle had been fired precisely at quarter past two.

Saran was the first on the scene, followed quickly by Percy Thorn and Greeves. Greeves and Saran were fully dressed—a fact which no one but Donovan seemed to note. It was Saran who switched on the lights.

"What has happened?" he cried, his voice oddly loud and forced.

Donovan pointed at the huddled form lying on the floor, the head and face of which were hidden by the large collar of the dressing gown as the body had slumped to the floor.

"Murder!" he replied.

Saran looked bewildered, and as Greeves came running up, his eyes were wide in astonishment and incredulity, but they were not looking at the body on the floor—they were fixed on Macklin Donovan.

Mrs. Glassock now came from her room, and behind her was Genevieve, while servants were pouring from the upper floors.

"Who is it?" demanded Percy Thorn.

Donovan stooped and drew back the collar of the dressing gown.

A scream broke from the lips of Mrs. Glassock.

"My God!" she cried, "it's Mason."

"Father!" exclaimed Percy Thorn, dropping to his knees beside the body. "Who could have done it?" he cried. "Who could have done it?" and he looked around at them all standing there—questioningly, accusingly.

Donovan knelt beside Percy and turned the body over on its back, opened the dressing gown and the shirt and placed his ear above the heart. Presently he arose. They were all looking at him, eyes filled with suspense. Donovan shook his head, sadly.

"Mr. Thorn is dead," he said. "Greeves, go to the phone and call the police. Percy, we shall have to leave the body here until they come. You had better go and prepare your aunt, and prevent her coming down until after the police have been here. I shall remain here. The rest of you may go to your rooms or not, as you wish. There is nothing that anyone can do until after the police come."

Percy Thorn came to his feet like one in a trance and moved slowly down the hall toward the stairs leading to the third floor, where was his aunt's room. Greeves ran quickly down the stairs to the library to the telephone. Donovan looked about him. Where was Nariva Saran?

"Mrs. Glassock," he said, turning to that lady, "will you kindly step to Miss Saran's room and see if she is all right."

Mrs. Glassock crossed the hall and knocked lightly on Miss Saran's door. There was no response. She knocked again, more imperatively. Still no response.

"Try the door," directed Donovan.

It was locked.

Donovan turned toward Saran. "Where is your daughter?" he demanded. He was no longer the suave young society man. Instead, his voice cut like steel, and in it was the ring of steel.

Saran was pale. "She must be in her room," he replied. "Where else could she be?"

Donovan motioned to a couple of frightened footmen. "Break down the door!" he commanded.

As they stepped forward to obey, the door of Nariva Saran's room opened, revealing her standing there, fully dressed and breathing rapidly. At sight of

Macklin Donovan, she voiced a little cry that she tried to smother, and her eyes went very wide.

"What has happened?" she cried, when she found her voice. "I heard a noise—I must have swooned. Who is it?" and she looked down at the still figure on the floor. "Oh, no!" she cried when she recognized the features, "it cannot be—it cannot be Mr. Thorn—it must be a terrible mistake!"

"It was a terrible mistake, Miss Saran," said Donovan coldly, his eyes steadily upon hers.

CHAPTER III

Mystery

The strato police ship came, and, as Fate would have it, under the command of Lieutenant Terrance Donovan. The body of Mason Thorn was removed to the small room off the library—a room that he had used for a study and in which was a large couch. He was laid upon the couch, near an open window.

Then Terrance Donovan returned to the library. Mrs. Glassock was there, and Genevieve. Trying to comfort his aunt, Percy Thorn sat on a sofa beside her, as she wept softly. Saran stood before the cold fireplace smoking a cigarette. Greeves remained beside the door to his master's study. There were three burly police officers and some of the maids and housemen also, the latter standing near the hall doorway as though momentarily expecting to be banished.

"Now," said Terrance Donovan, "I want to hear about this. Who saw the shooting,"

"No one," replied his son, "as far as I have been able to discover. The killing occurred at precisely a quarter past two." He glanced at Saran, but the latter was looking at the ceiling. Nariva was not in the room. "I was the first to reach the hall. I found Mr. Thorn lying where you found him, but on his face. It was necessary for me to turn him over to examine him for signs of life—otherwise the body was not disturbed."

Neither Lieutenant Donovan nor Macklin had given any indication of their relationship or that they were even acquainted, owing to the fact that the latter was assuming a role necessary to the successful prosecution of his investigation and that exposure at this time would doubtless nullify all that the Department had accomplished.

"Who do you think might have had reason to kill Mr. Thorn?" continued Lieutenant Donovan.

"I believe that no one could have had any reason for wishing to kill him," replied Macklin. "To my knowledge, he hadn't an enemy in the world, and I never heard him in altercation with anyone—" He paused. "It is my belief, sir, that the needle that killed Mr. Thorn was intended for another." As he spoke he looked directly at Saran, whose eyes were now upon him, and was rewarded by a slight narrowing of the other's eyelids. Somehow this chance shot had gone home. Saran knew something.

"Who followed you into the hall after the needle was fired?" asked the police official.

"I did," said Saran. "Mr. Donovan was standing over the body of Mr. Thorn as I came from my room. The hall was but dimly lighted, yet sufficiently to permit me to see Mr. Donovan. He was putting something in his hip pocket as I opened the door of my room."

The insinuation was obvious, and that it was thoroughly understood was manifest by the sound of quick intaking of breath by several of the occupants of the library.

Macklin smiled. "You'd better have me searched, lieutenant," he said.

"I object to his being searched or questioned farther by this officer," protested Saran.

"Why?" asked Lieutenant Donovan.

"Because you are his father," replied the Assurian.

The effect of this second surprise was almost equal to that of the first. The chin of Mrs. Peabody Glassock dropped for an instant, then she smiled superciliously.

"The count must have lost his mind," she whispered to her daughter. "The very idea—Macklin Donovan the son of a common policeman!"

Genevieve turned to a police officer standing behind them. "What is the lieutenant's name?" she asked.

"Terrance Donovan, mum," replied Officer McGroarty.

Mrs. Glassock appeared slightly groggy, but she was still in the ring. "Ridiculous!" she exclaimed "He is of the Donovans of San Francisco." She looked defiantly, and crushingly at Officer McGroarty.

"Sure, mum," said he, "an' it wasn't me that was after sayin' he wasn't—it was him over there," he nodded in the direction of Saran.

Terrance Donovan eyed the Assurian. "What makes you think this man is my son?" he demanded.

Saran hesitated. He seemed to regret that he had made the charge. He smiled deprecatingly and spread his palms before him with a shrug. "One of the servants at Three Gables told my valet. I gave the matter no thought—scarcely believed it, in fact, until you arrived here tonight. Then I recalled."

"How does it happen that you know my name?" asked Terrance Donovan.

Saran was evidently nonplussed by the question. He realized his mistake instantly, but it was too late to remedy it. He sought to cover his confusion by a show of anger.

"It makes no difference how I know," he snapped. "I *do* know, and I don't propose permitting the murderer of my friend to escape because he is the son of a police lieutenant. I demand that some other officer pursue this investigation."

Terrance Donovan nodded. "You are right," he said. "I think Captain Bushor is here now—I just heard his ship arrive."

"He does not deny that Macklin is his son," whispered Genevieve to her mother.

"Preposterous," said Mrs. Glassock, but she said it in a small voice—she was weakening. "I always mistrusted him," she added; "he never impressed me as one having the air of one to the manor born, as it were."

At this juncture, a large man in the uniform of a captain of police entered the room. He nodded to Lieutenant Donovan and crossed to his side. The two men whispered together in low tones for a few minutes, then Captain Bushor pointed a large forefinger at John Saran.

"Do you accuse Mr. Macklin Donovan of the murder of Mason Thorn?" he asked.

"I accuse no one," replied Saran; "I merely relate what I witnessed."

"What else did you witness beside what you have told Lieutenant Donovan?"

"After the police came, and while they were carrying Mr. Thorn's body down stairs, Mr. Donovan went to his room, took a piece of paper from his pocket and burned it."

Macklin Donovan looked at the speaker in surprise. Saran had spoken the truth, but how had he known?

"Perhaps," continued the Assurian, "he may have hidden his pistol at the same time—provided of course that it was he who shot Mr. Thorn. If the pistol is not in his possession now, it may be in his room. He should be searched and so should his room."

"Sure it's a dirty frame," grumbled Officer McGroarty. "I've known Mackie Donovan since we was knee-high to nothin' at all, an' there ain't a sneaky hair in his head." He spoke in a whisper that was audible only to the Glassocks.

"Then you admit that he is the son of that person there," accused Mrs. Glassock. "I am not in the least surprised. I have said right along that he had a low face."

Genevieve Glassock looked at her mother in wide-eyed astonishment. "I think he's wonderful," she said, "and I have changed my mind about marrying him." She could not resist the temptation to retaliate for the older woman's past unwelcome efforts at match-making.

"You will return to Philadelphia today," snapped Mrs. Glassock.

Captain Bushor was searching Macklin for a weapon—which he did not find.

"Now we'll take a look at your room," he said. "You come along," he pointed at Saran. "The rest of you stay here. See that no one leaves the room, McGroarty."

Lieutenant Donovan glanced quickly around the library as he accompanied Bushor, Saran, and Macklin toward the stairway.

"Where's the butler?" he demanded suddenly.

"Why, he was here just a moment ago," replied Percy Thorn. "Perhaps he's stepped into the next room," and he pointed to the study where his father's body lay. "Greeves!" he called, but there was no response.

One of the policemen stepped into the adjoining room.

"There ain't no one in there," he said.

"Find him," directed the captain as he led the way up the stairs, with Mackin Donovan at his side.

Upon the left of the landing half way up the stairs was a tall pier glass. Reflected in it, just for an instant, Macklin saw the shadowy figure of a woman dart into his room at the far end of the dimly lighted hall. He was upon the point of telling Bushor what he had seen when there flashed to his mind the realization that all the women in the house, save one, were in the library below, and that one was Nariva Saran.

An instant later they reached the head of the stairs in full view of the entire hallway. There had been no opportunity for whoever had entered his room to leave it. The hall had been lighted when last he passed through it after the officers had come, but now the lights were extinguished, the only illumination coming from the landing on the stairway. Who had extinguished them, and why? Possibly what he had just seen reflected in the mirror explained why.

The three men walked directly to Macklin's room, which, like the hall, was in darkness^ although Donovan distinctly recalled that the lamp on the reading table had been lighted when he left the room. Just inside the doorway was a switch. Macklin pressed this switch and the room was flooded with light.

"I suggest that you make a very thorough search," said Saran.

"When I want any suggestions from you, I'll ask you for 'em," replied Bushor tersely. Saran subsided, scowling.

"Got a gun, Macklin?" asked the captain.

"It's in my dresser—top drawer on the left," replied young Donovan, indicating the article of furniture with a jerk of his thumb.

Captain Bushor crossed to the dresser and opened the upper left hand drawer, in which he rummaged for a moment

"No gun here, Macklin," he said.

Macklin Donovan knitted his brows. "It was there at the instant that Mr. Thorn was killed," he said. "I had just placed it there."

The police officer continued to ransack the dresser, and then each of the other pieces of furniture in the two rooms and the closet. Nowhere could he find a pistol.

Saran was quite evidently restraining a desire to speak only with the greatest difficulty. At last he could hold his peace no longer.

"Why don't you search the bed?" he demanded.

Macklin glanced quickly toward the bed, the covers at the foot of which, he noticed for the first time, were disarranged, as though they had been pulled out from the side and hastily tucked in again. Bushor crossed to the bed and threw the coverings aside. One by one he removed and shook them. Finally he turned the mattress completely off the springs. Saran was almost standing on tip-toe. There was no weapon there!

Young Donovan was looking at Saran, upon whom he kept his eyes as much as possible, and he saw the look of blank surprise that crossed the Assurian's face.

All the time that the search had been going on, Donovan had been awaiting the discovery of the person he had seen enter the room only a minute ahead of them. As every nook and cranny was examined without revealing any hidden presence, he was reduced to a state of surprise fully equaling that which Saran had revealed when no pistol had been discovered beneath the mattress.

Walking to one of the windows, he looked out and examined the roof along the front of the penthouse—there was no one there, either.

They returned to the library just as the officer who had been detailed to find Greeves entered the room.

"I've searched the whole place, Cap'n," he said, "an' he ain't here. The penthouse is being watched outside, front an' back, an' there ain't no one gone out."

Bushor nodded. "Then he must be inside," he said. He turned to the company in the room. "You'll all admit that there's something peculiar about this case. I can lock you all up on suspicion, but I don't want to do that. Right now, there isn't a case against anybody, and so I'll give you your choice of remaining here under guard until morning or goin' to the station. Under the circumstances, I can't make any exceptions, and I'm stretchin' a point in lettin' you stay here. Which will it be?"

They unanimously chose to remain in the house under guard.

"Now go to your rooms and stay there," Bushor said.

He walked from the room, beckoning Lieutenant Donovan to follow him.

"I left 'em here," he explained in a low voice, "because I think here is the best place to trap the murderer. He's one of 'em, but I don't know which one. Don't let any one leave the house, and say, find that damned butler. See you about eight o'clock," and he departed.

CHAPTER IV

Ghostly Disappearances

As the guests started toward their rooms, Macklin found himself beside Mrs. Glassock and Genevieve. "It has been a terrible experience for you," he said. "I hope that it has no ill effects. If I can be of any service, do not hesitate to call upon me."

Mrs. Glassock's chin arose perceptibly. "The only service you can render us, young man, is to permit us to forget the humiliating position in which your imposture has placed us," and she swept majestically up the stairway.

Genevieve paused beside him. "I *am* sorry for you, Mr. Donovan," she said coldly, "but you brought it upon yourself. One should not pretend to be what one is not," and she followed her mother up the stairs to their rooms.

Percy Thorn, assisting his aunt, followed them. As he passed Donovan, he stopped and put a hand on the other's shoulder.

"I want you to know, Mackie," he said, "that I think Saran is a damned liar."

"Thanks," replied Donovan. "I knew you wouldn't believe such a ridiculous charge."

"But who in the world could have done it?" asked Thorn.

Donovan shook his head. "I wish I knew."

He remained a moment after the others had gone to speak to his father—to ask the latest news concerning his mother, only to learn that there had been no change, then he, too, ascended the stairs toward his room. As he reached the top step, the door of Nariva Saran's room opened and he saw her standing there. It was evident that she wanted to speak to him. She held a finger to her lips, enjoining silence, at the same time motioning him toward her. He had taken but a couple of steps in her direction when the door of Saran's room opened and he stepped into the hall. Simultaneously Nariva stepped back into her room and closed her door.

"I thought your room was at the opposite end of the hall, Mr. Donovan," said Saran, with a slightly sarcastic inflection.

"No one should know it better than you," replied Macklin.

Saran paled. "Keep away from my daughter's room," he said nastily.

Macklin bowed. "She has been absent from the library since the police came," he said, "and I feared that she might be indisposed. I but wished to stop and inquire. Perhaps you can enlighten me."

"My daughter is quite well, thank you," replied Saran, and as Donovan bowed again and turned toward his room, the other watched him until he was out of sight.

Again in his room, Donovan threw himself into an easy chair beside the table and sat pondering the occurrences of the night. That which occupied him most was a mad effort to discover some means of removing all suspicion connected with the attempt that he believed had been made upon his life by Nariva Saran. He did not want to believe it. Yet, try as he would to reach another, the conviction remained unalterable that she had attempted to lure him to his death, and that by chance only Mason Thorn had approached her door at the very instant she had expected Donovan.

It made him wince to even think it, and so he would set off each time upon a new tack in a fruitless effort to explain her various questionable actions upon some other hypothesis. But he could not explain away her evident surprise when she had discovered him alive; he could not explain why she had been the last to come to the hall after the firing of the fatal needle; he could not explain why she and Greeves alone of all the company had been absent from the library during the police investigation. His judgment told him that she and Greeves and Saran were at the bottom of the plot to kill him, yet just now when she had attempted to speak to him Saran had prevented it.

Then there was the memory of those almost tragic words. They still rang in his ears: "I do love you!" and recollection of the horror that had been in her eyes as she voiced the cry and fled up the stairway. What did it all mean?

Abruptly his eyes spotted the floor at the base of the closet door, beneath which a piece of paper was slowly being pushed into the room.

Cautiously, Donovan arose from his chair and tip-toed across the room toward the closet. He made no noise as he moved—none until his hand fell upon the knob and then, in the same instant, he flung the door wide. The closet was empty!

He entered it and examined every inch of it. It was absolutely empty except for a couple of suits that he had hung in it the day before. Like all the other closets in the house, it was wainscoted with cedar to the same height that the rooms were paneled in various orna-mental woods.

Hair prickling on his scalp, Donovan came from the closet and locked the door, leaving the key in the lock. Then he stooped and picked up the bit of folded paper. It bore but a single word—the same word that the other message had borne: BEWARE!

As he stood before the closet door turning the bit of paper over and over, he searched his mind for an expla-nation as to the means by which it had been shoved from under the closet door without someone being in the closet. Suddenly his attention was attracted by what seemed to be a shuffling sound from one of the balconies before the windows on the opposite side of the room.

Cautiously he raised his eyes. The light from the reading lamp illuminated the table, the chair beside it, and a little area of the floor surrounding the two, leaving the balance of the room in a subdued light.

Beyond the table was the window from which the sound seemed to come. As he watched, he thought he saw something move upon the balcony just outside. He remained very quiet, apparently examining the paper in his hand, his eyes barely raised to the window. Again he saw the movement without—a human hand clutching a weapon.

There was the hiss of a needle gun. The hand disappeared. The tinkle of metal on stone. A curse. Silence.

Donovan leaped for the window, threw it open, and stepped out onto the balcony. There was no one there—there was no one on any of the other balconies.

A rich Irish voice rose from below: "What the devil's wrong up there?" it demanded. Its owner was one of the officers left to guard the rear of the house.

"I thought I heard a noise," called Donovan. He said nothing about the figure on his balcony, for he had determined to ferret out the mysteries of that night unaided.

He stooped and examined the stone floor of the balcony. There lay a dagger. He picked it up and carried it into his room. He could hear people running through the hall, aroused and alarmed by this second disturbance. He heard the gruff, low tones of the police and the high, frightened voices of women.

He carried the dagger to the table and held it close to the light. It was a weapon of foreign make, its velvet grip bound with cords of gold. A faint fragrance wafted to his nostrils. Quickly he raised the grip closer and inhaled, then he let the weapon fall to the table as his hand dropped limply at his side. His face was drawn and white—the hilt was scented with Nariva Saran's perfume.

For a moment he stood thus, then he turned and walked quickly to the door, opened it, and stepped into the hall. He wanted to see who was there—or, more particularly, who was not.

They were all there—Saran, Nariva, the Glassocks, servants, and police. Percy Thorn came down a moment later, his aunt behind him. Greeves alone was absent. No one seemed able to know anything, and Donovan kept silent as to what had transpired upon his balcony and within his room.

Tired, haggard, and nerve-wracked, the occupants of the penthouse returned once more to their rooms. Macklin threw himself upon his bed, fully dressed, after switching off the lights. He did not intend to sleep. He wanted to wait until the place quieted, if it ever did, that he might, in comparative safety from discovery, go to Saran's door and listen. He had an idea that Greeves was there, and he wanted to make sure. But he was very tired—almost exhausted—and he dozed before he realized the danger. It could have been for but an instant before his sleep was shattered by a piercing scream.

Macklin leaped from his bed and ran toward the hall door. As he did so, from the closet door on the opposite side of the room a pistol hissed in the dark and a needle sang by his head. As he had no weapon, he could not return the fire, but he sprang to the switch and turned on the lights. Then he wheeled and faced the closet door. It was closed and the key was still upon the outside, where he had left it. He crossed the room and tried the knob—the door was locked!

Entering the hall again, he found it filled with nervous men and terrified women. Everyone was talking at once. Only the police were near normal, and even their nerves were a bit on edge.

Lieutenant Terrance Donovan was among them.

"Who's missing, Macklin?" he demanded of his son.

"The butler, John Saran, and Saran's daughter," replied young Donovan, looking over the crowd.

"The butler is not on the premises," said his father. "Which is Saran's room?"

"Here," said Macklin, leading the way. The others crowded in their rear.

Lieutenant Donovan opened the door and fumbled for the light switch. His son stepped past him and found it, flooding the room with light.

"Look!" he exclaimed, and pointed toward the closet.

There, on the floor, his body in the room, his legs extended into the closet, lay John Saran upon his back, blood running from a needle wound in his forehead. Macklin Donovan turned and ran toward the hall.

"Miss Saran!" he cried. "Something may have happened to her."

His father followed him, and again the others swarmed behind. Macklin knocked upon the girl's door—there was no response. He knocked again— louder. Silence. Motioning the others aside he stepped back, paused, hurled himself against the door with all his weight, striking it with a shoulder. The bolt and keeper tore through the wooden frame, and the door swung inward. A single lamp burned upon a table. The room was empty, as were the dressing room and bath and closet.

Macklin called the girl's name aloud: "Nariva! Nariva!" but there was no response. He looked blankly at his father. "What do you make of it, Dad?" he asked.

The older man shook his head. "It's got me," he admitted, "but we'll find her—she must be in the house."

"That's what you said about Greeves," his son reminded him, "but you haven't found him yet."

"I'll search the house myself this time," replied Terrance Donovan. "I want to have a closer look at Saran's room and the body, then we'll lock it up, and I'll go through the place."

Together they went into the hall and approached Saran's door. It was closed—they had left it open. The elder Donovan tried the knob, then he stooped and looked through the key hole.

"The door is locked, Mackie," he said. "Locked on the inside," he turned to one of his men. "Break it in McGroarty," he said.

The huge Irishman had to do little more than lean against the door to send it crashing into the room. The lieutenant smiled.

"There is nothing heavier than a ton of Irish," he said, and McGroarty grinned, but the smile and the grin both faded as the two officers stepped into the room, for Saran's body was not there—only a little pool of blood marked the spot upon the floor outside the open closet door where the dead man had rested.

Terrance Donovan scratched his head, then he turned and looked accusingly at the company clustered in the doorway. A wide-eyed, terrified housemaid was sobbing hysterically.

"Shut up!" admonished Donovan, whose own nerves were on edge by the various happenings in this penthouse of mystery.

"I c-can't," sobbed the girl. "If ever I lives through this night, I quits. The house is haunted. I've said so right along. The noises I've heard—my lord!"

"What noises have you heard?" demanded Lieutenant Donovan.

"Footsteps at night w'en I'd be a-comin' home late. I'd run all the ways up stairs as fast as I could go, 'til I got scairt to go out o' nights."

"Footsteps where?" asked the officer.

"In those rooms when there wasn't nobody in 'em—on this floor mostly. This floor's the worst."

"Didn't you ever tell anyone about 'em?" pursued Donovan.

"Sure! Didn't I tell Mr. Greeves half a dozen times?"

"What did he say?"

"He said I was just a nervous little girl afraid of the dark—that it was all my imagination. Imagination! I suppose poor Mr. Thorn a-lyin' downstairs dead, is imagination. An' this here dead man wot gets up an' locks his door an' vanishes—I suppose he's imagination, too. My lord!"

Donovan turned to the others. "If you would feel safer together," he said, "you may go to the library and remain there the balance of the night—it will not be long now until daylight. There are officers all around the penthouse—you will be perfectly safe there."

"I wouldn't go back to my room alone if you'd star me in the Television Follies," said the house maid. The others appeared to feel similarly, for they moved toward the stairway and down to the library in a huddled group. There were no stragglers.

CHAPTER V

The Vanishing Mr. Greeves

Lieutenant Donovan, with Macklin and McGroarty, searched the penthouse from top to bottom—there was not a room, or closet, or cupboard that they did not investigate—but their search revealed no trace of Miss Saran, the butler, or the body of John Saran. They had vanished as though they had never existed.

"It's got me," said Lieutenant Donovan.

Macklin shook his head. "There's some explanation," he said.

"Of course there is."

"And I intend to find it. Good night, Dad, I'm going to my room again."

The older man reached into a pocket and produced a needle gun. "Take this, Mackie," he said. "You may be needin' it. I found it in the library table. And I'm goin' to send a couple of the boys up to sit with you."

"What for?" demanded the young man.

"I can't be tellin' you, Mackie—you wouldn't understand—but I've got my own reasons, and they're good ones. I been puttin' two and two together this night—an' they don't make eight, either."

"I can take care of myself, Dad."

"Sure you can. That's probably what Thorn and Saran thought, too. Now look at 'em."

Macklin shrugged. "All right," he said; "but remember that I'm working on a case and tell them not to interfere with me."

"They'll be under your orders, my boy."

Shortly after Macklin Donovan entered his room the two police officers knocked at the door.

"Make yourselves at home, boys," he said as the two entered, and going to the table he brought cigars for them. "I don't want to talk," he said, after they |ad seated themselves and lighted their cigars, "I want to listen." They nodded.

Both the officers were sleepy and in a few minutes were half dozing. Macklin was listening and thinking. He was trying to figure some explanation that would account for the mysterious disappearance of two living inmates of the penthouse and a dead man. He attempted also to fathom the causes underlying his father's recent apprehension concerning his own safety. If Terrance Donovan had known all that had occurred in the house and especially in Macklin's room, there would be ample grounds for his fear; but he did not. He must know something else, then. What was it?

Both the officers were dozing, and Macklin was deep in thought when he was startled by a sibilant *"S-s-st!"* from somewhere at his right. He wheeled around, facing the two officers. Neither one of them had moved, and their deep, regular breathing attested the fact that both were asleep. In the middle of the floor, between Donovan and one of the officers, lay a bit of paper folded into a small cylinder and wrapped with a rubber band.

Donovan rose and stepped quickly to the window. There was no one on any of the balconies. Then he turned to the closet door, which he found still locked and the key on the outside where he had left it. He moved on tiptoe to avoid arousing the officers, and thus he investigated both his room and the bath. Finally he returned to the room where the policemen still slept and picked the piece of paper from the floor. As he unfolded it he expected to find the usual message— *Beware*—but this was something different.

"Be quick! Get out of this room. Your life is in danger," it read, in the same crude printing that had marked the others.

One of the officers awoke just as Macklin was stuffing the paper into his pocket.

"Anything wrong?" asked the policeman. "I thought someone was walkin' 'round the room, or was I sleepin'?"

"You were sleeping, all right," said Donovan, "and you can go back to sleep if you want—I'll watch."

"What's that?" whispered the officer, cocking an ear.

"Sounds like someone in Saran's room," replied Macklin in a low tone, at the same time moving cautiously toward the door.

The sound they had heard was a subdued crackling noise. Against the silence of the night, and coming as it did from the vacant room in which Saran had been murdered, it induced an impression of uncanniness that made both men shiver, inured though they were to dangers and to mysteries. Behind Donovan came the policeman, and as the former laid his hand upon the knob of the door, the other officer awakened.

Observing their silence and their stealthy movements at a glance, he arose and followed them with equal quiet. Together the three crept out into the hallway and moved noiselessly toward Saran's door, which stood open as it had since McGroarty had broken it in.

Macklin took the lead. He had reached the frame of the door and was on the point of looking into the interior of the room when a figure stepped from it into the hall. Instantly Macklin seized it—it was Greeves.

The butler was evidently surprised, but he remained cool.

"Beg pardon, sir," he said, "I did not see you."

"No," said Donovan sarcastically, "but I saw you. I've been lookin' for you, Greeves."

"Oh, have you, sir?" exclaimed the butler, in his best official tones. "I am very sorry, sir. I have been in my room."

"You're a damned liar, Greeves," exclaimed Donovan.

"Yes, sir!" replied the butler. "I was just looking for you, sir. You must not return to that room," and he pointed along the hall toward Macklin's door.

"Why?" demanded Donovan.

"It is not safe, sir."

"Why is it not safe?"

"I cannot tell you, sir; but please believe me, it is not safe," and then he turned to the officers. "Do not allow him to return to that room, I beg of you," he insisted. "Even if you remain with him, he will be a dead man within five minutes after he crosses the threshold."

Macklin Donovan stood eyeing the butler closely. The man was evidently very much in earnest, but what motives prompted the warning? Donovan had his own opinion—the gang wanted to keep him out of that room for some particular reason, and they were trying to frighten him out, first by the note and now by means of Greeves. Well, he wouldn't be frightened. He saw that the butler was out of breath and that his clothing was soiled here and there with dust and cobwebs.

"Where have you been all night?" he demanded suddenly.

"Attending to my duties," responded the butler.

"Once more, you are a liar."

"Yes, sir!"

"Where is Miss Saran?"

"Is she not in her room, sir?"

"Where is she? Answer me!"

"You will pardon me, Mr. Donovan, but I have other duties to attend to. I must be going," and he moved toward the stairs leading to the upper floors.

"No you don't!" cried Donovan, and he grabbed for the man.

Greeves dodged him and started to run.

"Get him!" cried Macklin to the officer who was nearest the butler.

The big Irishman jumped in front of the fugitive and held out both ponderous hands to seize him. It was a foolish move, for it left his chin exposed; but then who would expect a middle-aged butler to be so rough? Greeves struck the policeman once without even pausing, and as the latter slumped to the floor, the butler leaped across his body to the stairway.

Just as he turned into it, Macklin drew his gun and fired, at the same time leaping in pursuit with the second policeman at his heels. Macklin fired again as he reached the foot of the stairs and saw Greeves disappearing at the turn halfway up.

Donovan was young and active. He went up those stairs three or four at a time, but when he reached the top, Greeves was nowhere to be seen.

Followed by the officer, Donovan ascended at a run to the fourth floor—still no Greeves. He searched every apartment there and even found the scuttle that led to the roof, but that was fastened upon the inside, precluding the possibility that Greeves had escaped in this way, even had he had time to do so in the short interval of his lead over Donovan.

Crestfallen, the two men returned to the third floor and searched it thoroughly. They were joined there by Terrance Donovan and McGroarty, who had been attracted by Macklin's shooting. Young Donovan narrated the incidents of the last few minutes to his father.

"He just vanished—that was all—vanished," he concluded.

Donovan senior scratched his head. "As I've said about forty times this night, Mackie, it's got me, and I've been twenty-two years on the New York police force an' seen some funny things. If I hadn't pounded on walls tonight until I've near wore all the hide off me knuckles, I'd say the place was full o' phony panels, but it ain't—every wall's as solid as every other one—there ain't no air spaces nowhere. And then, too, boy, I've even paced off the length and breadth of the penthouse and the rooms and the closets, and there's no space unaccounted for. And there's no way into the tower below. Yes, sir—it's got me."

"It's getting me, too," said his son; "but I'm goin' to stick with it."

"You keep out of that room, though," said his father. "Better come down to the library with the others."

Macklin shook his head. "I'll go in the room across the hall from mine—that's not being used," he said.

"There ain't any of 'em being used except the library," remarked the lieutenant with a smile. "You can take your choice of a lot of rooms—but I wouldn't care for Saran's, myself."

"Nor I," said Macklin, "there's something funny about that room."

Together they descended to the second floor. "On your way down, turn the light on the landing out. Dad," said Macklin; "I want to listen up here in the dark for a while."

"Keep to your room," cautioned his father.

"If it's dark, they can't see me to harm me and I can listen from my doorway without being seen," explained Macklin.

"All right," agreed his father and walked down the hallway toward the stairs leading to the library, while Macklin and the two officers turned toward the room opposite that which young Donovan had occupied.

Macklin turned off the remaining hall lights, leaving the second floor in utter darkness. Then he entered the room with the policemen, switched on the lights there long enough for them to find chairs, and then switched them off again. Before their eyes could become accustomed to the darkness, he recrossed the room to the door and stepped out into the hall, making no noise. In equal silence, he crossed to the door of the room he had formerly occupied.

Stealthily he turned the knob and opened the door. The darkness within was solid except for the two rectangular spaces that were the windows—areas that were but faintly visible against the deeper darkness of the room.

As he stood just inside the door listening, he thought that he discerned something moving on one of the balconies—just a vague suggestion of a figure without definite form or shape. It riveted his attention and held his eyes. Very softly, he reached behind him and closed the door, fearing that one of the officers in the room across the hall, missing him, might switch on a light that would be sure to reveal him standing there in the doorway.

Drawing his pistol, he moved slowly forward toward the window—inch by inch he moved, fearing that the slightest noise might frighten away whatever haunted his balcony. He had crossed to about the middle of the room, when, without warning, the narrow beams of a flashlight burst from the closet full upon the window toward which he had been creeping.

Macklin Donovan came up short with a gasp as his eyes rested upon what the beams of the flashlight revealed beyond the window—a face pressed close against the pane—the face of Saran, the dead man, with the blood upon its forehead.

Almost instantly the face vanished toward the left, and then the flashlight swung slowly about the room, coming closer and closer to Macklin Donovan. Macklin's first impulse was to flee—there was something so uncanny about the silence and the seeming inevitableness of that grisly light searching him out in the darkness of the chamber of mystery. Then he sought to keep ahead of it, but at last it drove him into a corner, where he halted and held his pistol ready.

An instant later the light touched his face and stopped upon it, blinding him. Then it was that he raised his weapon and fired point-blank into its fiery eye. Instantly the light disappeared.

A moment of silence was followed by a weird crackling sound, coming, apparently, from the interior of the closet—then silence again. Donovan sprang through the darkness for the closet door. Fumbling for the knob, he found it; but the door was locked, and the key, which had been on the outside, was gone.

CHAPTER VI

The Mystery of the Closet

Slightly bewildered by the rapidity with which the events of the past few moments had followed one another, and dazed by the inexplicable mystery of the weird light that had blazed through the panels of a locked door, Donovan hesitated as he sought to adjust his reasoning faculties to the improbabilities of the facts that confronted them and select a plan of action.

Long since had the call of duty merged with an over-mastering urge to discover the fate or the whereabouts of Nariva Saran and to determine definitely her connection with the plotters, that he might fix her responsibility in the matter of the murder of Mason Thorn and the attempts upon his own life. Just how far she was involved with Greeves and Saran, he could not know, and now the shooting of Saran had helped to upset whatever theories he had commenced to entertain relative to the connection existing between the three.

If Greeves and Saran had been in league with one another, and there was no doubt in Donovan's mind but that they had been, it seemed unlikely that Greeves should have shot Saran, while the conclusion that Nariva had been guilty of the murder of her father was impossible of entertainment.

Who, then, had shot Saran? Was Saran dead? The fact that he had seen and recognized Saran's face at the window but a moment since would have, under ordinary circumstances, settled that question definitely; but the circumstances of the past few hours had been anything but ordinary.

Where was Nariva? If Saran were not dead, it was reasonable to assume that, if he could find him, he could find Nariva also, since the most natural conjecture would place father and daughter near one another. But where to search for them! They had not left the Thorn Building, yet they were not in the Thorn penthouse. Already had the place been searched until there remained no unrevealed hiding place where even a cat might have concealed itself successfully from the searchers. There remained but a single tenable conclusion—all others were preposterous, unthinkable, verging upon the demoniacal.

Sane judgment assured him that Saran was not dead—that the face he had seen at the window must have been the face of a living man, and that that man was John Saran. The thing to do, then, was to follow.

He walked quickly across the room, raised the window, and stepped out upon the balcony. The apparition, or the man, whichever it had been, had disappeared to the left, so toward the left Donovan looked. Three feet away was the balcony before the windows of the dressing room and bath, and beyond that, at similar intervals, the balconies of the adjoining rooms. Below was the small garden between the rear of the penthouse and the landing deck of the skyscraper, whereon rested two ships—the police ship and the Thorn ship. Nowhere upon the balconies nor in the garden was anyone in sight, though he knew that directly beyond were the policemen guarding the building's roof.

Stealthily, that he might not attract the attention of the officers, Donovan climbed over the hand-rail and stepped to the next balcony. There he paused for a moment, listening. He heard nothing other than the subdued night noises of the city from far below. A mile away loomed the twin tower, a giant searchlight sweeping the sky in ceaseless grandeur.

Cautiously he made his way to the nearest balcony. The window letting upon it stood wide open. Within lay darkness and silence.

He threw a leg over the sill and drew himself into the interior silently. His feet dropped softly to the floor and he stood erect. Eerily he sensed the room was not unoccupied. Of that he had startling proof immediately. From out of the darkness at his left came a low-toned whisper.

"Go back!" it warned. "In the name of heaven, go back before they kill you!"

For just a moment Donovan hesitated, then he turned and moved quickly across the room in the direction from which the voice had come. He walked with his left hand extended before him, in his right his needle gun.

"Who are you," he demanded, "and who will kill me?"

"S-s-st!" warned the voice. "They will hear you."

Before him a closet door opened, and he gazed blankly into its empty interior. It was lit with a dim radiance, seeming to glow from the very walls. Advancing cautiously, he entered, his weapon ready. The voice was no longer in evidence.

"Who is here?" demanded Donovan, his hair crawling on his scalp. "Where are you?"

There was no answer.

Donovan rapped with his knuckles sharply at the walls, but they were solid all around. His knocks gave forth no hollow sounds, only muffled solidity of tone. Several coat hangers caught his eye. In the odd glow that still permeated the place, like a sort of after-vision, one of them seemed to shine with a light all its own. He reached up, touched it. It seemed loose. He grasped it and pulled.

Instantly he let go. All about him a weird blue light shone, and a strange crackling noise came. A second, then it was gone, and he was plunged into utter darkness. Behind him the closet door was closed, and he backed hastily against it before he realized the fact. Bewildered he whirled, ready for a trap, and his hand shot to the knob.

The door was not locked. It opened under his thrust.

Simultaneously a door at the far end of the room opened, revealing the figure of a large man silhouetted against the doorway of a lighted room across a hall. Across the hall, a room that was not in the Thorn penthouse. A strange room!

"Is that you, Danard?" demanded the man in the doorway.

Beyond him Donovan caught a glimpse of several men and a woman, seated or standing about a table. At the gruff question of the man in the doorway, those who were facing him looked up, while the woman, whose back had been toward the door, turned around. Macklin Donovan caught but a fleeting glimpse of her face, as at the very instant that she turned a hand reached out of the darkness and powerful fingers seized his arm. He was jerked violently backward. His pistol was wrenched from his grasp and he heard the loud voice of the man in the doorway crying: "Answer me, damn you, or I fire!"

Then a door closed behind him and there came to his ears, faintly, the muffled sigh of a needle pistol. He tried to grapple with the man who was dragging him along, half backward, through the darkness, but the man was very powerful and the whole incident lasted but a moment before he felt himself swung violently around and pushed heavily forward into the dark, where he stumbled and then sprawled headlong to the floor.

As he fell two thoughts animated his mind—one was that he must lie very quiet for the purpose of deceiving his assailant into the belief that he was stunned, that he might thus take advantage of the other and overpower him—the other was the realization that the woman he had seen in that weird lighted room that seemed to exist in some other space was Nariva Saran.

It seemed to him that he had scarcely fallen before he heard footsteps in front of him, running toward him. He heard a door fly open, and with the click of an electric switch the outer room was flooded with light.

He leaped to his feet then to grapple with his assailants and as he faced them he uttered an oath of astonishment and stepped back in utter incredulity. They were the two police officers whom he had left but a few minutes before. He was in the closet of the room from the window of which he had stepped a minute or two since. And behind him, where had been a door through which he had just been thrust, was a blank wall!

The policemen looked at him.

"What happened?" asked one. "We thought we heard a scrap goin' on in here."

"No," replied Donovan, his mind whirling. "I was just looking for something in the dark and stumbled into this closet."

Donovan moved toward the hallway. Through the pall of mystery, a light was breaking. What it would reveal, he could scarce even guess, yet that it would illuminate several hitherto seemingly inexplicable occurrences seemed probable, and it might lead to complete revelations. It might also lead to deeper mystery, and there was even a greater chance that it might lead to death; but that was a chance that every man in the service expected to be called upon to face in the pursuance of duty.

In only one respect did the plan forming in his mind disregard the straight path of duty, and that lay in

his determination to carry it through alone, notwith-standing the fact that he might enlist the cooperation of an ample force of police to assist him. The passion he felt for Nariva Saran prompted him to formulate his plan in secrecy and carry it out alone.

Whatever she might be, however guilty of attempts upon his life, love demanded that he give her every chance, and that he could not accomplish if he shared his suspicions with the police, even though one of them were his father, for the best of policemen appear to assume all those under suspicion as guilty until proven innocent.

If he led them, as he believed he could, to her hiding place, they would arrest her with the others, and all would be thrown into jail. He must, if possible, first discover the degree of her guilt. If he found her guilty, he assured himself sternly, no consideration of love would deter him from carrying on along the straight path of duty.

As he moved toward the doorway, one of the officers pointed at the floor behind him.

"There's your gun," he said. "It must have dropped out of your pocket when you did the Brodie."

"Yes," agreed Donovan, as he turned and recovered the weapon, still further mystified by the fact of its return to him.

In the hallway, he met his father coming from the third floor and called him aside.

"I think I'm next to something," he whispered in a low tone. "Don't ask me any questions. I'll tell you what I want and then you tell me if you'll do it."

"Shoot," said Lieutenant Donovan.

"I want every light above the first floor shut off and a stall made that will kid anyone who may be listening into believing that all of you have gone downstairs. But instead post three or four men in this hall, in the dark, and have one close to each of the doors on this side— mine, Saran's and his daughter's, with orders to nab anyone who comes out unless they give a countersign that we'll agree upon."

"How can anyone come out when there ain't nobody in any of these rooms?" demanded Terrance Donovan.

"I don't know," replied his son. "That's what I want to find out. The countersign can be Three Gables. Whisper it and all your instructions to your men—if walls ever had ears, it's these walls."

"What are you goin' to do?" asked the father.

"Never mind—I told you not to ask me any questions."

The older man shook his head. "Mackie," he said, "there's something about all this night's business that I've got a hunch is hooked up with something I can't tell you about, yet. If I'm right, it's all got more to do with you than it has with Mason Thorn. I wish you'd get out of this house an' go home. I'll send a couple of the boys with you."

Young Donovan laughed.

"I supposed you'd laugh," said his father, "but I wish you'd do it, Mackie. I don't think your life's safe here."

The younger man placed a hand affectionately on his father's shoulder. "Don't worry, Dad," he said, "I can take care of myself, and even if I can't, you don't want a son of yours running away from his post, do you?"

Lieutenant Terrance Donovan turned slowly away. "The lights'll be out an' the men posted in two minutes," he whispered, "an' God be with you!"

In less than the brief time he had stipulated, the upper floors of the penthouse were in darkness, and Lieutenant Donovan, with several of his men, was descending to the first floor with considerable show of noise, so that any listener might think a greater-than-actual number was descending. Behind him, he left three burly policemen silently guarding three doorways in the blackness of the second-floor hallway.

CHAPTER VII

Across Space

Donovan stood still until after the lights had been extinguished, then he crept noiselessly through the darkness toward the room where he knew lay the road to that strange place of a world within a world, of rooms where no rooms were in this solid, real world of which he now was a part. He reached it and entered softly, his gun ready. The closet door he found closed, and his heart throbbed as he laid a hand on the knob.

It was like placing a hand on the knob of a door that led to infinity. Beyond was a space no more than four feet square, and yet, it opened into an unseen universe. But where?

Nariva Saran was there, and where she was, he wanted to be, to prove to himself, at least, her innocence or her duplicity. Whatever it was, he must know the truth.

Abruptly, he turned the knob and opened the door. The interior of the closet was black as ink. No dim bluish radiance now of a weird encroaching world. No ghostly radiation from nowhere.

An eerie sense of appalling danger gripped him as he nerved himself to step over the threshold. Was anyone lurking there, ready to kill? But he reasoned it was just as dark to anyone else, and if they were there, he had an equal chance.

He stepped forward, waved a hand about—four walls, all blank! The closet was empty. He released the pent-up breath in his lungs and closed the closet door behind him. Then his searching fingers sought the hangers on the wall. He found one, rested his fingers lightly upon it, his body suddenly chill. There, beneath his hand, lay the unknown. Some weird science should spring out as he pulled it down.

Stiffening, he pulled suddenly. Nothing happened. The hanger did not move. No dummy, this, but the real thing. He felt for another, found it, and once more pulled it down. It gave, and abruptly the weird blue light sprang forth. A second of time he had to observe it, hear its uncanny crackling sound, then it winked out. As simple, as quick as that!

Eager now for action, he turned to the door. But he halted abruptly as he heard muffled voices from beyond. They seemed far away, as though more than one door intervened. Cautiously he turned the knob and opened the door a fraction of an inch. The voices came louder now, raised in altercation. But the room beyond was dark and empty.

Opening the door wide, Donovan advanced across the room, conscious of its strangeness. Beneath his feet was no carpet, as had been the case beyond the closet of the room he should have been in. It was a bare floor, uncarpeted, of stone.

He found a door, ajar, leading into a hallway and slipped through it. Here was light, dim, coming from outside through several windows and a partly transparent glass wall. Passing a window he gazed out in all-consuming curiosity. Would a glimpse of the familiar roof-top of the Thorn building, the gardens beneath the tiny balconies, give him a clue as to the location of these rooms and halls?"

But at the sight that met his eyes, he gasped aloud. There was a roof-top, but a strange one. And beyond its rails was New York, as he had always seen it, with its giant skyscrapers. A mile away loomed a giant one—and his heart failed within him as he recognized it. It was the Thorn Building!

"Great God!" he whispered.

He, Macklin Donovan, had been transmitted in an instant of time across a mile of space, to the twin tower he had looked upon so many times already this night! Incredible, fantastic occurrence! What weird science was back of it all? What great thing had he stumbled upon? No petty attempt on a millionaire's money, this, but something colossal, something far ahead of the science of even that great city out there.

The beat of angry voices broke through his amazement now, and he realized with a start what his mission was. Here, in this giant building of mystery, was Nariva Saran. And somehow, he knew now, she was a helpless tool in the grip of strange sciences.

He came to a door. Beyond it were the voices. He listened.

A man was speaking—the voice coarse and uncultured. He spoke in the Assurian tongue. Young Donovan understood it well, and he was glad now that his father had insisted upon his learning it. He had never understood why so much stress had been laid upon languages in his education—he did not understand now. He merely was glad that he had learned Assurian as well as French, Spanish, and German.

"There is a traitor among us," the man was saying.

"Or Thorn divulged the secrets of the penthouse to others," suggested a second voice. "That, you know, is very possible and would explain much."

At the sound of the second voice Donovan raised his eyebrows, for he recognized the tones—they belonged to Greeves.

There was some grumbling, as though of dissent from the suggestion, and then the first voice spoke again. "This girl—how long have you known her, Saran? There is something about her that reminds me of someone else. Are you very sure of her?"

"You ought to be sure of me—I have been working with you for more than a year," said a feminine voice. It was Nariva!

"The Committee recommended her," came a man's voice—Saran's. "Beyond that, I know nothing of her. Until tonight I have had no reason to mistrust her; but now! By God, someone is double-crossing us— someone tried to kill me. She is the only one who could have had a motive."

"What motive?" demanded the gruff voice of the first speaker.

"The fool is in love with him."

There was a long silence and then, suddenly, an exclamation from him of the coarse voice. There was the scraping of a chair and other sounds indicative of a seated man rising excitedly to his feet.

Donovan kneeled and placed an eye close to the key-hole, revealing, in the thus circumscribed range of his vision, three of the occupants of the room.

Seated at a table, her back partially toward him, Nariva Saran was nearest the door beyond which he knelt; upon the opposite side of the table from her he could see two men. One of them was Saran, who, seated, was looking up at the man at his right—the one whom Donovan had heard rise from his chair. The latter, a coarse, heavy man, leaned forward across the table and shook a trembling finger in the face of Nariva Saran. He appeared inarticulate with rage.

Donovan could not see Greeves, nor the other occupants of the room—if there were others—except a man's hand and part of a coat sleeve resting on the table to the right of the bearded figure. There might be a dozen men in the room, for aught that Macklin Donovan knew to the contrary, and he sincerely hoped that, however many constituted the gang, they were all in that room—it would have been most embarrassing to have had one of them come up behind him at that moment.

He wondered what it was all about—the obviously overmastering excitement and anger of the man facing Nariva Saran—the trembling, accusing finger—the tense silence of the others in the room.

Presently the bearded one found his voice.

"Spy!" he screamed. "I know you now!"

He turned excitedly to the right and left toward the others in the room. "You are fools!" he cried. "We are all fools, dupes. The scientists have tricked us nicely. Do you not know who she is?" His voice rose almost to a shriek, as he turned upon the girl again. He leaned so far forward that his pudgy finger almost touched her face as he pointed it at her.

"You are Sanders' daughter!" he cried.

"Think of it," he exhorted the others, "the daughter of Michael Sanders, the acknowledged war leader of the scientists, admitted for more than a year to our inner circle."

He turned upon the girl again.

"You deny it?" he demanded.

"Have I denied it?" she asked. Her voice was level, her mien dignified; but Donovan could see that her cheek was pale.

"You know the fate of spies?" the man continued.

The girl nodded. The man faced Saran.

"The responsibility for this is more yours than another's," he said. "Is it possible that there are two spies among us?"

"There may be two, Danard; but I am not one of them," replied Saran, whose facial muscles were working in nervous anger. "She tricked me, as she did all of you; but she did not try to kill any of you. She tried to kill me, the—" he applied a foul name to her. "For the safety of the cause, she must die. Let me, then, be her executioner."

Danard held up a restraining hand. "Let this thing be carried out in order," he said. "Have you anything to say, Spy?"

"What could I say to you, Danard, betrayer of the Science Ruler's trust, murderer, exploiter of your fellow country-men, traitor, that would influence you from the decision that you reached the instant that you recognized me. I am ready tonight, as I have always been, to die for Assuria and the science empire."

"Then die!" cried Danard, flushing angrily, and nodded to Saran.

The latter rose and drew a pistol from his pocket. The girl rose, too, and stood facing them haughtily, her head high.

At the same instant, just as Saran raised his weapon, Macklin Donovan pushed the door aside and stepped into the room. The secret-service-man fired first. Saran grasped at his breast, slumped forward upon the table, and then slipped to the floor.

The other occupants of the room whirled toward the intruder—there were five men and the girl.

Danard uttered an exclamation of surprise as recognition came to him.

"Ah!" he exclaimed, "it is he!"

"Who?" demanded another—"not—?"

"Yes," cried Danard—"Alexander!" And then: *"For Assuria! For the New Freedom!"* he screamed and leveled his needle pistol.

Donovan raised his own weapon and pulled the trigger—with no result. The empty shell had jammed after he had shot Saran.

Simultaneously, Greeves drew a gun and fired, dropping Danard in his tracks.

Nariva leaped past Macklin to the switch beside the door and plunged the room into darkness. Someone grasped him by an arm on one side, and an instant later he was seized by a second person upon the other.

Danard was groaning.

A voice cried: *"Stop them! Kill them!"*

There was the sound of heavy shoes on stone floor, and furniture pushed about and overturned. Nariva's voice sounded in Donovan's ear.

"Come quickly!" she whispered. "You can trust me—you *must* trust me!"

He felt himself rushed along through the darkness, turning first this way and then that. Then he felt hands seize him from out of the darkness ahead, and he collided with an invisible form.

"Halt!" commanded a deep voice, and then. "I got 'im; give a hand here."

Heavy footsteps sounded, running. An instant of flickering, crackling blue, then more darkness. Then someone switched on lights, and the astonished Donovan found himself in the second floor hallway of the Thorn penthouse, a burly policeman grappling with him, while two more came running to the assistance of the first. On one side of him was Nariva Saran, and on the other, Greeves.

The officer who held him looked hurt. "Why didn't ye give the counter-sign?" he demanded.

Terrance Donovan, leaping up the stairs from the library three at a time, came down the hall at a run.

"Hang on to those two," he ordered, indicating Greeves and the girl. "Good boy, Mackie, you got 'em! That's the boy!"

"I didn't get them, though," replied young Donovan, ruefully; "they got me."

Greeves was smiling. "You needn't worry about us now, Lieutenant Donovan," he said. "We won't elude you again—there's no more need for it."

"I'll say you won't!" exclaimed Terrance Donovan; "not if I know myself, you won't. I've got you now, and I'm goin' to keep you."

"There's something about this, Dad, that we don't understand," said Macklin. "Greeves and Miss Saran just saved my life. But before we go into it any farther, we've got to get the rest of the gang." He turned to Greeves. "Will you show Lieutenant Donovan and his men how you get back and forth between these two buildings so easily and so quickly?"

"Certainly, sir," said Greeves, "but I doubt if you find your men now. We got the ones who counted. The other three were only tools working for hire, and, as far as I know, they have committed no crimes."

"Who in hell are you, anyway?" demanded Macklin Donovan of the butler.

"Wait until we come back and I will tell you everything," replied Greeves.

"Go ahead, then," commanded Lieutenant Donovan, "but I'll keep a good hold on you—you may be all right but you're too damned slippery to suit me."

Greeves laughed. "All right, Lieutenant, I don't know that I can blame you," he replied.

"Mac, you stay here and see that this woman don't get away again," Terrance Donovan instructed McGroarty, "the rest of you come along with us."

Greeves led them into the room formerly occupied by Macklin. The closet door now stood open, as the lights revealed after Greeves had switched them on. Crowding them all into the closet, the butler closed the door, took hold of a hanger at the end of the closet, and pulled on it.

The blue radiance flared. Although nothing seemed changed, Greeves opened the door, leading them into a chamber corresponding with the one they had left, except that it was unlit. He switched on the lights, revealing an unfurnished room.

"My God!" rasped Lieutenant Donovan, leaping forward and staring out of the window. "Where are we, and how did we get here?"

"You are in the penthouse of the tall building a mile from the Thorn building," Greeves explained. "And you have just been transmitted by means of radio waves from a closet inside the Thorn building to this room. The apparatus is built into the walls. Assurian science has gone far in twenty years."

Lieutenant Donovan, clearly startled, glanced at his son. "Yes." he said slowly. "It has!"

The police crossed the hall, entered the room, and switched on the lights. Saran's dead body lay upon the floor, where it had fallen. With the exception of a few pieces of furniture, some of which were overturned, the room was vacant and unoccupied.

Greeves frowned. He turned to Macklin Donovan.

"I thought Danard was mortally wounded," he said. "I expected to find him dead."

Donovan nodded. "The others must have helped him get away, but they can't be far. You'd better search, Dad."

"You'll find a trap door leading to the building proper," Greeves told them, "but it will be useless to follow. They've gotten away by this time. It's too bad we lost Danard—he's the man you want."

"Why?" demanded Lieutenant Donovan.

"It was Danard who murdered Mr. Thorn."

CHAPTER VIII

A Prince of Science

As Macklin Donovan entered the Thorn library a few moments later with Greeves, Nariva Saran, and his father, he spoke pleasantly to the Glassocks and the Thorns. Percy Thorn returned his greeting cordially. Miss Euphonia, crushed and weeping, was too buried in her own grief to notice anyone. Genevieve Glassock nodded indifferently and looked in another direction, while Mrs. Peabody Glassock, looking directly through him, failed apparently to perceive either him or his salutation, unless a slightly increased elevation of her patrician chin denoted aught to the contrary.

"It is strange," she whispered later to her daughter, "that the Thorns should have tolerated such people; but then poor Mason could not have known. It is Percy's fault—he must have gotten it from his mother; her grandfather, you know, had nothing—absolutely nothing. Ah, blood will tell—always! One can see it in that Donovan person—common, very common."

She was interrupted by Lieutenant Donovan's gruff voice. "Now, Greeves," he was saying, "if you've got anything to say, I want to tell you first that it may be used against you."

"I understand," replied the butler. "In the first place, Lieutenant Donovan, it may help you to understand matters better from the first if I tell you that this young lady," he indicated Nariva Saran, with a respectful inclination of the head, "is not the daughter of Saran. She is the daughter of Michael Sanders, twenty-two years ago War Minister of Assuria, whom, doubtless, you well recall."

Terrance Donovan's face betrayed the astonishment the statement induced.

"As you know, the Alexander of Assuria was brought to America in infancy to preserve him from the wrath of the revolutionists, who assassinated the balance of the science family the day following his removal from the palace. Only Sanders and the Science Ruler's valet, Paul Danard, beside yourself and your wife, held the secret of the whereabouts of the boy.

"Danard joined the revolutionists, but he kept his secret until recently, using his knowledge to extort money from Sanders, the head of the scientist's party. For the past three years he has been the infamous power behind the infamous government that has reduced Assuria to bankruptcy and starvation.

"Recently the power of the scientist party has increased tremendously, until it now constitutes the hope of Assuria and the only menace to the criminal coterie that has for so long held the fate of the country in their bloodstained hands.

"The hope of the scientists lay in the young Alexander, though only a few knew that he still lived, and only one scientist, Michael Sanders, knew where and under what name and disguise. But Danard knew, too, and we have been watching him closely.

"For that purpose, Nariva and I gained access to the councils of Danard and his fellows. We learned that Danard had conceived a great ambition, and to further it he brought together the malcontents from all parties and formed them into the so-called New Freedom Party. A *coup d'état* was planned for next month, when the present government was to be overthrown and a new one proclaimed, with Danard provisional president. The next step was to be a dictatorship, following which Danard was to seize all the reins of government, announce an empire and crown himself Science Ruler of Assuria.

"There was every possibility for the success of his bold play. The greatest obstacle lay in the existence of the rightful heir to the science throne—Alexander would constitute an ever-present menace to his power. Danard, therefore, determined to search out young Alexander and kill him; but Danard was clever. Really, he trusted no one, and made no confidants. Until tonight, not even we who were closest to him realized his true intentions.

"His party consisted of many factions, all of which must be appeased. He claimed, therefore, that he was coming to America to find Alexander and to prevail upon him to return to Assuria as the first president of the new science republic, thus winning the confidence of both the lukewarm scientists who had joined his forces and the out-and-out Freedom advocates as well.

"Nariva and I were sent by the true scientists to watch him, for Sanders, naturally, feared the man's every motive. We had the greatest difficulty in locating Alexander, due to the fact that his present calling is such that he was forced to assume an identity different from that which we were told would reveal him to us. None of us knew him by sight—not even Danard, while the young man himself is ignorant of his true identity.

"We have searched for months. Tonight we found him. Danard got the first clue yesterday morning, but said nothing to us. Saran clinched it a few minutes after Mr. Thorn was murdered, as did I, though I think Danard may have told Saran earlier in the night—that, I do not know.

"Lieutenant Donovan, I do not need to tell you who the heir to the science throne is, nor the gratitude that every true Assurian owes you for your faithful service to Science Empire. I should like to be the first to salute my future ruler, but there is one who better deserves that honor," and once again he turned and bowed to Nariva. "As her father has given his fortune, so she has dedicated her life and risked it many times for the sake of the Scientists of Assuria."

Nariva smiled and inclined her head toward Greeves, then she turned to Macklin Donovan and, curtsying low before him, took his hand in hers and raised it to her lips.

"Sir, I salute you!" she said.

Donovan grasped her arm and raised her to her feet. His face was flushed with embarrassment. He drew her close to him and threw an arm about her waist, as he turned toward Greeves.

"What is the meaning of all this idiocy?" he demanded.

"It is the truth, Your Majesty," replied Greeves. "Lieutenant Donovan can assure you of all that."

"I think you've all gone crazy," snapped Macklin Donovan, "and anyway, all this has nothing to do with the business that interests me now—who murdered Mason Thorn, and why? There is a great deal more to be explained, Greeves. I want the history of the past few hours—not the history of Assuria."

"Very well, Majesty."

"Cut the 'Majesty'!"

"Yes, Maj—yes, sir!" assented Greeves with a smile. "Yesterday morning you were followed to and from Lieutenant Donovan's home. That was evidently Danard's first direct clue as to your identity. He thought you a spy employed by the scientists. When he found who you really were, he told us that he had discovered that you were about to expose us to the United States government. Of course, such a step would have effectively ruined all his plans. He said you must be killed.

"Nariva and I tried to warn you, though we had no idea who you really were. Saran forged the note that was slipped under your door, and that was to lure you to your death. Poor Mr. Thorn chanced to pass through the hall at the instant you were expected, and the bullet that was intended for you killed him. It was fired by

Danard from Nariva's closet, which is also a radio-transmitter of matter.

"Nariva realizing that you were to be shot, hastily printed a note of warning, passed back through Saran's closet to the other building and thence to your closet, in which there is a small lookout panel, which opens as a slide. When you went to your dressing room, she entered the outer room and placed the note on your table, where you discovered it.

"After she left your room to return to her own, she heard the shot and thought it was you who had been killed. She screamed.

"Saran, too, thought that you had been killed. Possibly he showed surprise when he discovered that it was Mr. Thorn whom Danard had murdered by mistake, for he certainly must have been surprised and shocked too, since Mr. Thorn was to have financed the stroke that they expected would result in giving Assuria a new government."

"What did my father have to do with it?" demanded Percy Thorn.

"Your father was very much deceived. He thought that he was aiding mankind with his money, but he was only playing into the hands of unscrupulous tricksters. I do not know all that they told him, but you may be sure that little or none of it was truth."

"Go on with the story of what happened here this night," directed Terrance Donovan.

"Well, Nariva had difficulty getting back to her room without being observed by Danard, and she only did reach it just as you were about to have the door broken in. She was sure you had been killed, Mr. Donovan, and she told me that she almost betrayed herself when she discovered you alive.

"After you all went to the library, she returned to the other building to watch Danard and the others. It was in the library that I at last realized your true identity for I knew that the reputed son of Lieutenant Donovan was in reality Alexander of Assuria. I immediately hastened to the other building and acquainted Nariva with the facts.

"She had just learned something else from one of Danard's men. Immediately after Mr. Thorn had been killed, Saran had gone to his room as had most of the others and from there he had entered Mr. Donovan's room by the outer balcony and hidden Mr. Donovan's needle pistol beneath the mattress. Nariva barely had time to reach the room and remove the weapon before the police searched it.

"At last we determined that we must tell you of your danger, but when Nariva attempted to do so in the hallway, Saran discovered her and interfered. From then on he was suspicious, and we had difficulty in even getting the little notes of warning to you.

"Saran attempted to reach your room and stab you to death with a dagger belonging to Nariva. I tried to shoot him from an upper window, but succeeded only in knocking the dagger from his hand.

"Then, a few minutes later, Nariva discovered that Saran was planning to enter your closet and shoot you from the small panel. It was then that she shot Saran from his closet as he was about to enter it on his way to your closet.

"To shield herself, she ran to Danard and told him that one of the police had killed Saran. As there were papers on his body that Danard did not want to fall into the hands of the police he sent men to bring Saran's body to the other building. When they had done so it was discovered that Saran was only stunned by a scalp wound, and he soon recovered.

"At the same time that Saran was shot, Danard was in your closet waiting for Saran. He heard the shot, feared interference, and fired at you through the panel in your closet door. He did not wait to note the effect of this shot, but transmitted to the other building.

"The last time we warned you, Saran was on his way again to get you. Nariva had to throw the note from the closet of your room. At the same time, I made my way to Saran's room, determined at last that I must tell you face to face of your great danger. It was then that you caught me, sir.

"There is not much more to tell that you do not already know. You nearly killed Nariva when you fired at the light shining from your closet. She had been hiding there, expecting either Saran or Danard, or both, to come again in search of you. She dimly discerned someone on the balcony and turned the light upon them—it was Saran, as you know. The light frightened him away.

"Then she turned the light on you to make sure that it was you and not Danard. When you fired at her, you missed her head by scarce an inch, and she transmitted herself, fearing you might fire again. She had already removed the key from the outside lock by the simple expedient of reaching through the small aperture in the door—the same one through which Danard fired and that she used to shine the flashlight on Saran and you.

"When you followed Saran, it was I who dragged you into the closet and then hustled you to your own room in the Thorn penthouse.

"I guess that is all, Lieutenant," Greeves concluded. "I have tried to cover every point, and now won't you explain to—ah—er, his majesty, who he really is?"

"Wait a moment," said Terrance Donovan. "Not so fast. A week ago I could have told him, for I thought I knew. Now I'm damned if I know. We got a letter from Michael Sanders then. It told me something about his fears of a plot to assassinate Mackie, and for us to watch him very close as the time was almost ripe for him to return to Assuria.

"When I read the letter to my wife, she fainted, and when she came out of the faint she suffered a stroke. She has only rallied partially a couple of times since, and then she told me something that I don't know whether to believe or not, when the condition of her mind is taken into consideration. She kept cryin', 'I can't let him go—my little Mackie, my little Mackie!' And then, just in broken bits, she told me that he is our son—that it was Alexander who died on the stratosphere liner comin' over, an' I always thought that it was our own boy that died."

Greeves appeared dumbfounded.

"Can we not go to your wife at once and explain the necessity of knowing the truth," he insisted. "The fate of Assuria hangs in the balance—the happiness and prosperity of countless millions of people."

Lieutenant Donovan hesitated. "She is close to death's door," he said.

"But your promise to the Science Ruler!"

"Very well, we will go," he said, "but whether we shall question my wife or not depends upon the decision of the doctor."

It was already daylight when they entered the aerial taxis that had been summoned to take Terrance Donovan, Greeves, Nariva and Macklin to the bedside of Mrs. Donovan. The police lieutenant and Greeves occupied one of the cabs, Nariva and Macklin the other. As they drove off, Mrs. Peabody Glassock turned to Percy Thorn with a sickly smile.

"And to think," she said, "that you have been entertaining the future Science Ruler of Assuria without suspecting his true identity! But really, didn't you notice, Percy, his distinguished and majestic mien? Quite noticeable and very impressive."

In the second cab Macklin Donovan and Nariva sat in silence that was presently broken by the man.

"Before I knew who you were, I told you that I loved you," he said.

"Before I knew who *you* were, I told you that I loved *you*," she replied; "but now we must forget all that. You see how impossible it is."

"If I am a Ruler, nothing should be impossible. If I am only Mackie Donovan, the son of an Irish policeman, though, that will make the difference, for how could such aspire to the hand of a War Minister's daughter?"

"I pray to God you are only Mackie Donovan, dear," she whispered, "for then I can show you how easy it is to win her."

He took her in his arms. "Prince of Science or Mackie," he said. "I'm going to marry you."

www.ingramcontent.com/pod-product-compliance
Lightning Source LLC
Chambersburg PA
CBHW022049170626
46808CB00003B/1414